CW01003837

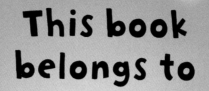

This book belongs to

· ·

First published 2020 by Brown Watson
The Old Mill, 76 Fleckney Road
Kibworth Beauchamp
Leicestershire LE8 0HG

ISBN: 978 0 7097 2894 8
© 2020 Brown Watson, England
Printed in India

Bedtime
Two Minute Tales

Brown Watson

ENGLAND

Contents

The Perfect Present

Copper lived in the enchanted forest with her fairy friends. All the fairies agreed that Copper was the friendliest, most-helpful fairy in the forest. She loved to look after everyone and make sure they were happy and healthy.

It was nearly Copper's
birthday. Usually, Copper
was in charge of finding
the perfect present for her
fairy friends, but now it
was Copper's turn to get
a present. Copper closed
her eyes and wished for a
brand new daisy necklace.

The forest fairies got together and thought about where they could get the perfect daisy necklace for their friend. 'I know just the shop!' said Dolly. 'If we go now, we'll be back in time for Copper's birthday party.'

13

But, just as the fairies were about to set off, a big rainstorm started. 'Oh no!' cried Dolly. 'Fairies can't fly in the rain, our wings will be too wet. What will we do now?' The fairies all huddled together to think of a plan.

When the rain cleared,
the fairies realised they
wouldn't have enough time
to go to the necklace shop.
Just then, the fairies looked
around them and saw a
patch of real daisies...

Dolly and her fairy friends gave Copper a daisy chain for her birthday. Copper loved it. 'It's just what I wanted!' she said. 'And it's even better because it was made by my very best friends.'

Narwhal's Magic

Deep in the ocean lived a beautiful creature called a narwhal. Eddie was a narwhal. He could swim fast like the dolphins and loved exploring the deep. But Eddie was most proud of his long narwhal horn.

Eddie's grandma told
Eddie stories of how his
horn was magical. 'Just like
a unicorn on land,' said his
grandma. 'Your horn can
do magical things...'
Eddie couldn't wait to tell
his friends. But they
weren't convinced.

'Your horn isn't magical!'
they laughed.
'All narwhals have them!'
Eddie was determined to
prove them wrong. 'Watch
this!' he said, pointing his
horn at a rock. 'I'll change
it into a beautiful seashell!'
But, as hard as he tried,
Eddie couldn't change the
rock into a seashell.

Eddie swam home as fast as he could to talk to his grandma. 'Our horns aren't magical at all!' he cried. 'I tried really hard, but my magic wouldn't work!' Eddie's grandma chuckled. 'Of course it wouldn't!' she said.

Eddie was confused, but his grandma explained. 'Narwhal's can only do their magic in secret,' she said. 'And only ever in front of other narwhals. Try again.' Eddie smiled and pointed his horn at a rock. He concentrated very hard, until…

...the rock started to shimmer and suddenly changed into a beautiful seashell!

'It's true!' he said. 'We really are magic!' Eddie didn't mind that he could never show his friends. Knowing that he was magic was enough for him.

Unicorn Club

Fern stared at a colourful letter that had just arrived in the post. It was from *The Unicorn Club*. They wanted Fern to be their newest member. But Fern was worried.

Fern had bright green hair.
Most of her unicorn friends
had pink or purple hair.
Although her mummy
thought her green hair
was beautiful, Fern wasn't
so sure. 'What if the other
unicorns make fun of me?'
she said.

On her first day at *The Unicorn Club*, Fern's mummy decided to walk her through the forest. 'Look at all the beautiful things in this forest that are green,' said Fern's mummy. 'The trees, the bushes, even that little bird. They all love being green.'

But Fern did not feel better. 'All of those things are meant to be green,' said Fern. 'I've never seen a unicorn with bright green hair before.' Just then, Fern saw another unicorn walking in the forest. She had bright red hair.

When Fern and her mummy finally arrived at the Unicorn Club they saw lots of unicorns with bright, colourful hair just like hers! Fern was delighted.

'Welcome to *The Rainbow Unicorn Club!*' said a unicorn with dark blue hair.

41

'*Rainbow Unicorn Club?*'
Fern repeated.
'Why yes!' said the unicorn.
'We are a club for unicorns
with hair that is all the
shades of the rainbow.
We LOVE your green hair.'
Fern smiled. She had to
admit, she loved her green
hair, too.

The Fiery Mountain

Dinks, Ella and Monty were bored. They had eaten all the fresh leaves they could find, and been swimming in the lake, but now they couldn't think of anything to do. 'There is one thing we could do...' said Monty.

Dinks and Ella looked worried. Whenever Monty had an idea, it was sure to lead them into trouble. 'We could go in search of the fiery mountain!' Monty said. 'Oh no!' said Dinks. 'I've heard it's far too dangerous!'
But Ella smiled. 'Come on, Dinks!' she said. 'It might be fun!'

Dinks sighed. She was still a little frightened of finding the fiery mountain, but she didn't want her friends to think that she wasn't fun. Slowly, she followed Ella and Monty through the trees, along a dark path.

Soon, the sky turned a
dark shade of red and
the air became thick with
smoke and heat.
'Th… that's it,' said Monty,
trembling. 'It's… it's very
big,' said Ella, shaking.
'And very… very fiery,'
said Monty.

51

Dinks smiled at her friends.
They didn't look so excited
anymore. 'Maybe you
were right, Dinks' said
Ella, turning to walk back
through the forest.
'Yes,' replied Monty.
'I'm sure we can find
something just as fun to
do back home!'

Bella's Breakfast

It was Mummy's birthday and Bella wanted to do something extra special for her. Mummy was always doing nice things for Bella. She took her to ballet lessons and to the park, and she even taught her to make cakes.

Bella decided that Mummy could do with a rest, so she got up extra early to make her a special breakfast. She got the tea pot and a teacup, a plate and a bowl. The only thing missing was... the food!

First, Bella tried to make her
mummy some porridge,
but it went hard and lumpy.
Next she tried to fry some
eggs, but they burnt and
went a funny shade of grey!

59

'Grey eggs and lumpy porridge. That's not going to show Mummy how much I love her,' Bella sighed. Just then, her Aunt Carly came in and saw all the mess. Bella explained what had happened.

Aunt Carly smiled. 'You wanted to do something nice for your mummy?' she asked. Bella nodded, sadly. 'But I haven't done anything nice at all,' she said. 'That's not exactly true...' said Aunt Carly.

Together, Aunt Carly and Bella climbed the stairs to Mummy's room and carefully opened the door. Mummy was fast asleep! 'You've given your mummy a nice long lie in,' said Aunt Carly. 'I think that's the best present of all...'

William the Wizard

William loved magic.
He wished more than
anything that he could be
a real wizard one day. So,
when William was given a
magic set for his birthday,
he was very happy. 'I'm
going to be the greatest
wizard, ever!' he said.

After William had tried some of the tricks in his box, he started to get bored. He wanted his wand to be real. Maybe, if he squeezed his eyes shut and wished really hard, his wand would make some real magic?

Just then, William's little brother came into the room. 'What are you doing?' he asked, when he saw his brother's eyes closed tight. 'Nothing,' replied William. 'You're not STILL playing with magic are you?' he asked.

71

William's little brother tried to take the wand out of William's hand. All of a sudden, the wand started to crackle. Sparks flew out of one end. Then, there was a loud bang! When William opened his eyes, his brother was nowhere to be seen.

'Down here!' said a tiny
voice. William looked down
and saw that his brother
was now the size of a mouse!
'What did you do?' said
William's little brother
(who now really WAS a
little brother).

William gazed at his wand in amazement. Had he really just shrunk his brother using real magic? 'William!' William jumped when he heard his mum calling from downstairs. If she found out what had happened, William would be in big trouble.

'William!' said William's mum again. 'It's time to get up!' William shook his head and looked around his room. Was it all a dream? He thought, staring at the magic wand on his bedroom floor.
'Morning!' said William's little brother, running into his room. William had never been so happy to see him.

The Best Kart in the Race

Annie was a racer. She was the best racer in her school. In fact, she was the best racer in her town. Annie won all the races she entered her little kart into, but now she was about to face her biggest challenge.

The Champion of Champions race took place each year. All the best karts from miles around took part. Annie had been too scared to enter before, but this year, she knew she was ready.

When Annie lined her kart
up with the rest of the racers,
she suddenly felt worried.
Everyone else's kart looked
so much newer and shinier
than hers. She searched the
crowds for her mum.

'Mum, I don't think I can race,' Annie said. 'All the other karts look amazing!' Annie's mum smiled. 'That's true,' she said. 'They LOOK amazing, but how do they race?' Annie was confused. 'I don't know…'

Annie's mum took her back to the starting line. 'Exactly,' she said. 'You won't know which kart is the best, until you race. What matters is the racer, not what the kart looks like.' Annie nodded and jumped into the driving seat.

Annie raced just as fast, and even faster, than some of the shiniest karts in the race. She came in second place and knew that she would be back next year to win – and she would do it in the same kart, too.

92

The Lost Robot

Ben, Christopher and Russ were brothers. Ben and Christopher loved to play adventure games. They would climb to the top of tall trees and explore the darkest corners of the garden looking for bugs.

Russ, however, did not like adventure games.
He preferred to kick his football or read a book.
Ben and Christopher thought their baby brother was a scaredy-cat. That was, until something strange happened...

The boys discovered a robot in their back garden! 'It must be someone's toy,' said Ben, excitedly. 'I wonder what cool tricks it can do?' said Christopher. 'I. Am. Not. A. Toy,' said the robot. Ben and Christopher jumped!

'It's an alien!' cried Ben.
'No, it's a monster robot!'
cried Christopher.
Russ sighed at his brothers
and calmly said to the
robot: 'Are you lost? Can
we help you?'
'Yes. Please,' said the
robot. 'Need. To. Return. To.
Robot. Family.'

Russ thought for a
moment. 'A clever robot
like you is sure to have a
button to tell your family
where you are,' he said.
'Yes!' replied the robot.
'It. Is. The. Green. One.'
Russ pushed the button
and the lights on top of
the robot's head started
to flash.

Soon, a whole family of robots appeared.

As Russ waved the robots goodbye, Ben and Christopher came out of their hiding place. 'You've just had a real adventure,' said Ben. 'And you weren't afraid at all,' said Christopher. From that day, they never called Russ a scaredy-cat again.

Good Boy, Bingley

It was a beautiful day, so Joey and her dad decided to walk their dog, Bingley, to the top of the hill to have a picnic. They packed apples and drinks, and Joey's favourite... jam sandwiches.

As they sat on the rug and got out the picnic food, Bingley began to sniff around, excitedly. He loved food. Especially everyone else's food. 'Sit down, Bingley!' said Joey's dad.

But Bingley couldn't resist. He found a juicy red apple and ran away with it in his mouth. 'Bad dog, Bingley!' said Joey's dad. 'That apple is NOT for you!' Bingley dropped the apple and went to sit by a tree, feeling sad.

109

Finally, Joey and her dad could sit down and enjoy their picnic. Just then, they heard a low, buzzing sound. Bingley was not the only one who wanted to share the picnic food...

A swarm of bees were heading straight for Joey's jam sandwiches! 'Help!' cried Joey, as she tried to bat them away. Just then, Bingley came rushing over. He barked at the bees until they flew away.

'Good boy, Bingley!' said Joey's dad. 'It's a good job you were here.' Joey filled a plate with Bingley's favourite dog treats, and together they had the most wonderful picnic, ever.

The Lonely Frog

Francis loved living at Lily Pad Pond. There were plenty of flies to eat, cool water to swim in and, of course, lovely lily pads to sit on. He was friends with the fishes and the birds, but there was one thing that worried him.

Of all the creatures in the pond, Francis was the only frog. He couldn't swim as fast as the fishes. He couldn't jump as high as the birds could fly. No matter how much fun he had with his friends, he always felt a little different.

One day, Francis heard a rustling in the reeds that surrounded the pond. 'Excuse me,' said a voice Francis had never heard before. 'What is this place?' Soon, another little frog pushed her head through the reeds.

'This is Lily Pad Pond,'
said Francis, happily. 'It is
where I live.'
'Oh,' replied the frog.
'My name is Frannie. I was
looking for a pond to live
in, but if this one is full, I'll
just hop along.'

123

Francis's heart leapt. At last he had found a froggy friend. 'No!' he cried. 'This pond isn't full. Well, it's full of nice fish and birds, but I'm the only frog and there are plenty of lily pads to go around.'

Frannie smiled. 'Thank you!' she replied.

The Witch Switch

Agatha was a very clever witch. She was so clever, in fact, that she had completed all the spells in her spell book. 'I want to try harder spells!' she told her mother one day.

'You can, when you're older,' replied Agatha's mother.

Potions
Level 2

Agatha didn't want to wait until she was older to try out some new spells. She wanted to learn, now! She snuck into her big sister's bedroom and found her spell book. 'Right, let's try this out!' said Agatha.

Agatha flipped to one of the hardest spells in the book and started to fill her big sister's cauldron. She took out her wand and whispered the special magic words. All of a sudden, there was an explosion of purple bubbles!

131

'What on earth are you doing?' said Agatha's sister, Agnes.
'I wanted to try one of your spells, but it went a bit wrong...' looking at the cat and mouse.
Somehow, Agatha's spell had switched their heads!

Agnes laughed. 'Agatha, what were you thinking?' she said. 'You have to learn how to use magic slowly, or things like this will happen!' Agatha nodded. 'But what about our poor cat?' she said, sadly.

Agnes took her wand out and waved it over the cat and the mouse. They instantly changed back to normal. 'When you are my age, you'll learn a reversing spell,' said Agnes. 'Would you like me to teach it to you?'

'No thanks!' said Agatha. 'I'll wait until I'm a bit older!'

The Penguin Slide

The littlest penguins in the colony had an exciting day planned. They were all going on a trip to the ice slide. Everyone was busy chattering away excitedly as they waddled to the slide. All, except one.

Soon, they arrived at the slide. It was very long, and very slippy, and it threw the little penguins high into the air before they sploshed into the water. The penguins lined up to take their turn, but little Penny wasn't happy.

When it was time for Penny's turn, she stood aside. 'You go,' she said to a bigger penguin behind her. 'I...I'm not quite ready.' The bigger penguin smiled. 'Don't worry,' he said. 'It's a bit scary at first, but then it's lots of fun!'

Penny shook her head.
'I don't think I can do it,'
Penny replied. 'But it does
look like fun.' Just then, the
bigger penguin had an
idea. 'I know what we can
do!' he said. 'Jump on my
back and we'll slide
down together.'

Penny nervously climbed onto the penguin's back. Together they zoomed down the slide. 'That was fun!' cried Penny.

When Penny got to the top of the slide for his second turn, she didn't hesitate. Sliding was super fun after all!

Fairy New Year

It was time for Fairy New Year. It was one of the best days of the year. All the fairies from miles around gathered to celebrate a new fairy year.

But something was wrong. Usually there were tables full of cakes for all the guests to share. Eating cake on Fairy New Year was a tradition. 'Oh no!' thought Clove. 'I wonder what has happened?'

'The fairy cake baker is poorly,' said Sunshine.
'I guess we won't have any cakes this year.'
Clove shook her head. Surely there was something they could do? No cakes on Fairy New Year just wasn't right!

Clove darted into her little house to think. Clove did what she always did when she needed inspiration. She sang her favourite song. Soon, her little bird friends had joined her. 'Why don't you use the enchanted toadstools?' they said.

Clove thought this was a wonderful idea. She searched the woods for the special, enchanted toadstools. She gathered them up and waved her magic wand over them. 'Enchanted mushroom soft and sweet, turn into something good to eat!' she said.

Soon, each of the mushrooms had turned into a delicious cake. There were sponges and chocolate cakes and, of course, there were plenty and plenty of fairy cakes. The Fairy New Year's celebrations could begin at last.

The Missing Crown

Princess Maddie loved to ride Poppy the unicorn through the forest. When it started to rain, Maddie and Poppy decided to ride home. Just then, Maddie realised her crown was missing!

As soon as the rain had stopped, Maddie and Poppy began to search the forest. They flew high above the treetops, looking for the glittering crown. It was nowhere to be seen.

Down below, a little rabbit called Honey had an idea. 'I think I know where the princess's crown has gone,' he said to his friend Sophia the squirrel. 'I think the naughty fairies have taken it, but we'll have to be very brave to get it back!'

Honey was right. The naughty fairies HAD taken the crown. 'This is ours now!' said Scrunch, the leader of the naughty fairies. 'Princess Maddie will never get it back!'

Just then, a group of good fairies flew by. 'We saw what happened,' they said. 'Scrunch and her friends can't resist a cake. We'll distract them with this one while you grab the crown!'

While the naughty fairies rushed to grab their cake, Honey and Sophia quietly took the crown. The good fairies and Honey and Sophia were all far away before the naughty fairies realised what had happened!

Maddie was very happy
to have her crown back.
She thanked Honey and
Sophia, and gave each of
the fairies a big hug.

The Lighthouse Mermaids

Southwater Lighthouse had been guiding ships at night for over 100 years. The lighthouse keeper and his son, Jonny, were very proud. They always kept the light shining.

One night, there was a terrible storm. The ships would need the lighthouse more than ever. But then, something terrible happened. The lighthouse light went out! Jonny and his dad knew what they needed to do...

The mermaids who lived in Southwater Bay had seen the lighthouse light go out. They quickly dived to the bottom of the ocean to fetch a glowing shell. The magic shells of Southwater Bay were the reason the lighthouse light always shone.

'Thank you,' said Jonny as he took the shell from the mermaid. He quickly handed it to his dad who took it to the top of the lighthouse. Soon the light was shining again. The mermalds clapped with joy before disappearing under the waves.

181

Jonny and his dad sighed with relief. The lighthouse was shining again thanks to the mermaids. Not only were they the Southwater Bay lighthouse keepers, they were the mermaid's secret-keepers, too.

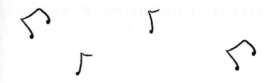

Betty's Dance Show

Betty loved to dance. She would jump, and spin, and hop. She could dance for hours and hours. So, Betty decided to join a dance class. At first, Betty loved it. The costumes and the dance studio were perfect.

However, after a while, Betty started to get fed up of following the dance teacher's instructions. 'Point your toes, Betty!' said the teacher. But Betty didn't want to point her toes.

187

DANCE
COMPETITION

SUNDAY 24th
May at 2pm

Soon, it was time for the annual dance competition. 'Please can I enter?' Betty asked her teacher. 'Betty, you are a very good dancer,' said her teacher. 'But if you can't follow the rules, you won't win!'

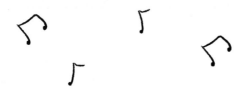

'I will!' pleaded Betty.
'I promise!' Betty's teacher
sighed. She wasn't sure
Betty was quite ready for
the competition, but she
said yes. Soon the day
arrived and Betty lined up
on stage with the rest of
the dancers.

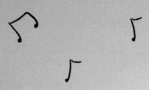

The music started. Betty's teacher was delighted as she watched Betty dance just like all the other girls on the stage. They were very good and soon it was time for the judges to announce the winner.

'We have a draw!' said the judge. 'One dancer from each team must perform a freestyle dance!'

Betty gasped. 'What does freestyle mean?' she asked her teacher. Betty's teacher smiled. 'It means you can do whatever you want!'

At last! Betty had the chance to show off her dancing doing any move she liked. She jumped, and span, and hopped. By the end of her performance it was clear who the winner would be. Betty had won the day!

The Archery Contest

Princess Sammy liked lots of things about being a princess. She liked her sparkly crown and her new dress, but best of all she loved playing with her bow and arrow.

One day, Princess Sammy told the king and queen that she was going to enter the archery competition. 'But, that's miles away!' said the king. 'Through the dark forest!' added the queen. Sammy wasn't scared. She was determined to go.

If you must go,' said the king. 'Make sure you take extra care not to bump into the scary dragon in the woods.'

Sammy smiled. She didn't believe in dragons.

Sammy strolled through the woods, thinking about the competition. She was sure she was going to win. Just then, she heard a rustling in the leaves. She tried to ignore it, but there it was again…

Just then, a dragon jumped out from behind the dark trees. Sammy was so shocked, she dropped her arrows and they all snapped in two. 'My arrows!' Sammy cried.

'Oh! I am sorry,' said the dragon. 'I didn't see you!'

207

'How will I compete in the archery contest without arrows?' said Sammy.
'I can help,' said the dragon. He picked up some spare twigs from the ground and used his sharp claws to turn them into new arrows.

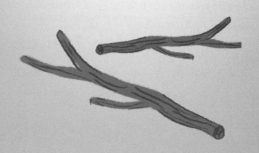

Soon, Sammy had lots of new arrows. 'Hop onto my back and you won't be late,' said the dragon. Sammy was excited about the archery competition, but she was even more excited to tell the king and queen they need never be frightened of dragons again.

The Kite Fight

Megan and Charlie were best friends, but they were always trying to outdo each other. If Megan got a new ball, Charlie would get a bigger one. If Charlie learned how to ride a bike, Megan would learn to ride faster.

One day, Megan arrived at the park with her brand-new kite. It was red and yellow with ribbons all along the string. She was just about to start flying it when Charlie arrived, too. He had a brand-new kite as well!

The kites looked exactly the same, but the two friends were each determined to prove that their kite was the best. Megan flew her kite first, then Charlie flew his right alongside it.

Megan pulled on her kite's strings and made it swoop this way and that. Charlie did the same and soon their kites were tangled together! They landed with a crunch on the floor between the two friends.

219

'I'm sorry about your kite,'
said Megan.
'I'm sorry about your kite,'
said Charlie.
'I was just showing off,'
said Megan.
'So was I,' said Charlie.

Just then, Megan had an idea. She started to pull the pieces of the kites apart. 'We can make a new kite,' she said.
'If we use the pieces from both our kites it will be twice as good!'

Soon, Charlie and Megan were flying the biggest, best kite in the whole park. They each held onto the string and realised that it was much more fun when they played together, instead of against each other.

Nancy's Rocket

It was an exciting day for Nancy. She had completed her astronaut training and was about to be given her very first rocket. 'Well done!' said BeeBoo, a little alien friend she had met on a recent visit to Jupiter.

227

'Thank you,' replied Nancy.
'Now, you had better hide,
my new rocket will be here
any minute!' BeeBoo zoomed
off, and Nancy waited.
Soon, her rocket arrived,
but it wasn't quite what she
expected.

Nancy stared up at her rocket. It was very big, and very shiny, but it was also very plain. 'Erm, excuse me,' said Nancy to the astronaut who had delivered it. 'I thought rockets were more colourful?'

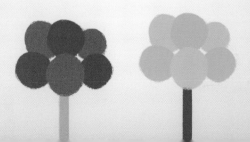

'Oh yes!' said the delivery astronaut. 'But it is a tradition that a new astronaut paints their first rocket themselves. Here you go!' The astronaut handed Nancy a pot of bright pink paint.

'Oh no!' thought Nancy. 'Not PINK, that's my least favourite colour!' Nancy didn't know what to do. She had waited for her first rocket for a long time, but she didn't want to fly around the galaxy in a pink one!

Just then, BeeBoo
appeared again. 'I just
wanted to see your new
rocket!' she said. 'What's
the matter?' Nancy
explained about the paint,
but BeeBoo just grinned.
'That's not a problem!'
said BeeBoo

Just then, BeeBoo whizzed the pink paint out of Nancy's hand and swirled it around the rocket. When she was finished the rocket was all the colours of the rainbow. 'It's perfect!' cried Nancy. 'Thank you!'

239

Starlight vs Albert

Starlight was a clever fairy. She lived in the enchanted forest and spent her days granting wishes and making magic potions. Albert was a talented wizard. He lived in the castle next to the forest, and often came looking for magic ingredients.

Although they were both good at magic, Starlight and Albert were not good friends. Albert thought Starlight was a nuisance, always getting in the way when he was collecting things for his spells.

243

Starlight thought Albert was always stomping around, disturbing the fairies' work. They were often found arguing in some corner of the forest.

'You are in my way!' shouted Albert.

'You should stay in the castle!' shouted Starlight.

One sunny morning, Albert was setting off to the forest in search of toadstools for a new spell, when something green caught his eye. Something large. Something green and very large. A dragon!

Albert tried to use his magic to stop the dragon, but it wasn't strong enough. The dragon breathed out fire and flew away towards the castle! 'I must stop it before it reaches the King and Queen,' he cried.

Albert ran into the forest, there was only one person he knew who could help. 'What do you want now?' asked Starlight. 'I need you to help me defeat a dragon!' pleaded Albert. 'You are the most powerful fairy I know!'

Together, Starlight and Albert combined their magic and sent the dragon far away. 'Thank you,' said Albert. 'I won't disturb the forest again.' Starlight smiled. 'I will help you find what you need, next time,' she said. 'It looks like we work well, when we work together.